CCJC

8/01

Editor's Note

An alphabet is a set of symbols. If the symbols were different from the letters we know would they still spell words? In this unusual ABC book, colorful shapes make up the alphabet, and a sturdy fold-out key is included to help readers decipher the word puzzles on each page. One clue: each word is the name of an animal, and the twenty-six different letter combinations are in alphabetical order. Do the shapes spell out ape? ant? bull? bear? cat? cod? A fun game, *Abstract Alphabet*, also serves as a terrific discussion starter on language and communication and will inspire readers to create imaginative alphabets of their very own.

For a guide to using this book with children,
please visit our website: www.chroniclebooks.com/Kids.

To Léopold, Ellsworth, Jean & Tony —P.C.

Copyright © Editions du Seuil, 1997.
First published in France as *Animaux*.
All rights reserved.

Book design by Paul Cox and Jessica Dacher.
Typeset in Futura.
The illustrations in this book were rendered in stenciled gouache.
Printed in Hong Kong.

Library of Congress Cataloging-in-Publication Data
Cox, Paul, 1959-
Abstract alphabet : a book of animals / by Paul Cox.
p. cm.
ISBN 0-8118-2940-5
1. Animals—Juvenile literature. 2. English
language—Alphabet—Juvenile literature. [1. Animals. 2. Alphabet.] I.
Title.
QL49 .C694 2001
428.1—dc21
00-011179

Distributed in Canada by Raincoast Books
9050 Shaughnessy Street, Vancouver, British Columbia V6P 6E5

10 9 8 7 6 5 4 3 2 1

Chronicle Books LLC
85 Second Street, San Francisco, California 94105

www.chroniclebooks.com/Kids

ABSTRACT ALPHABET

a book of animals

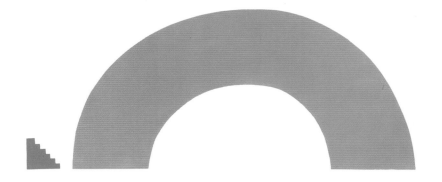

by Paul Cox

chronicle books · san francisco

B

C

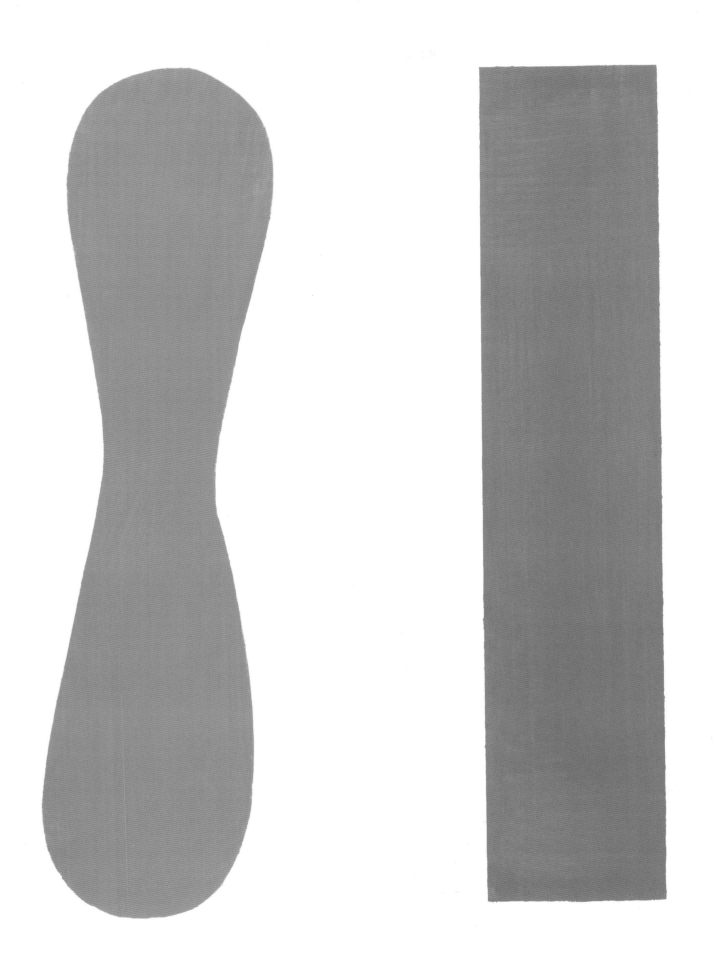

D

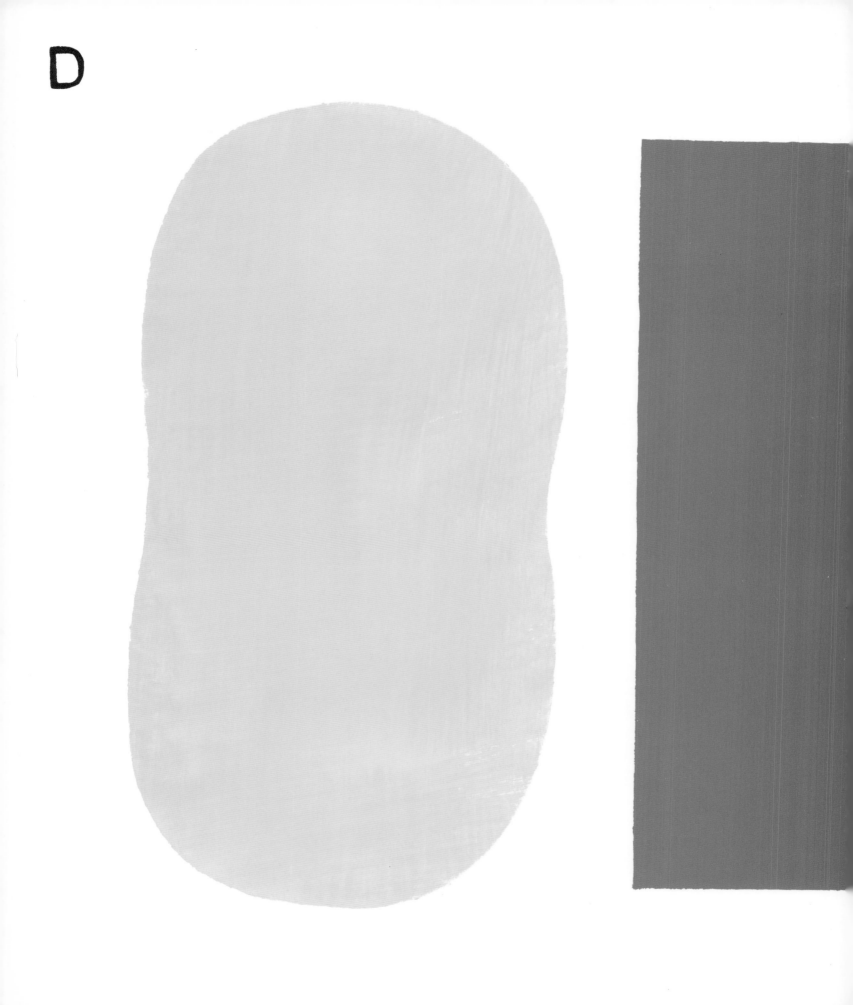

E

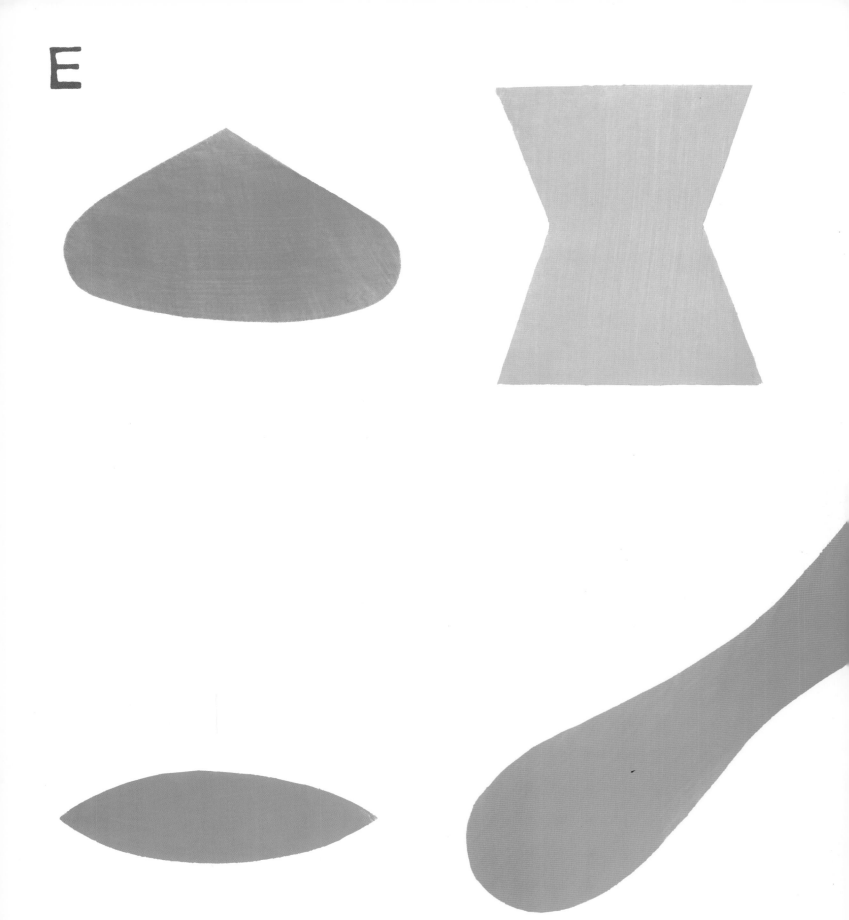

F

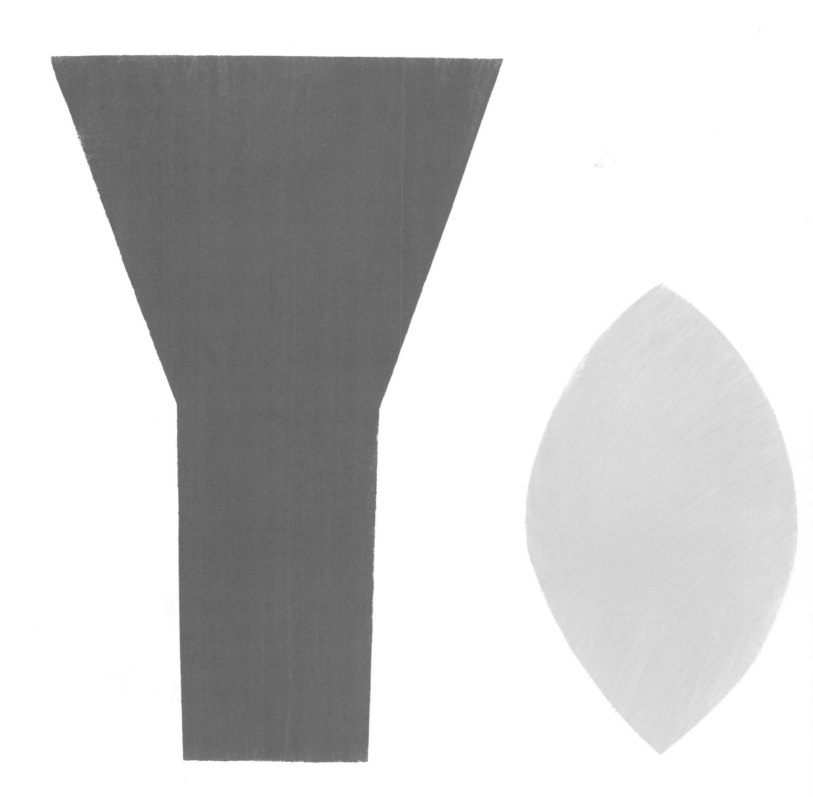

G

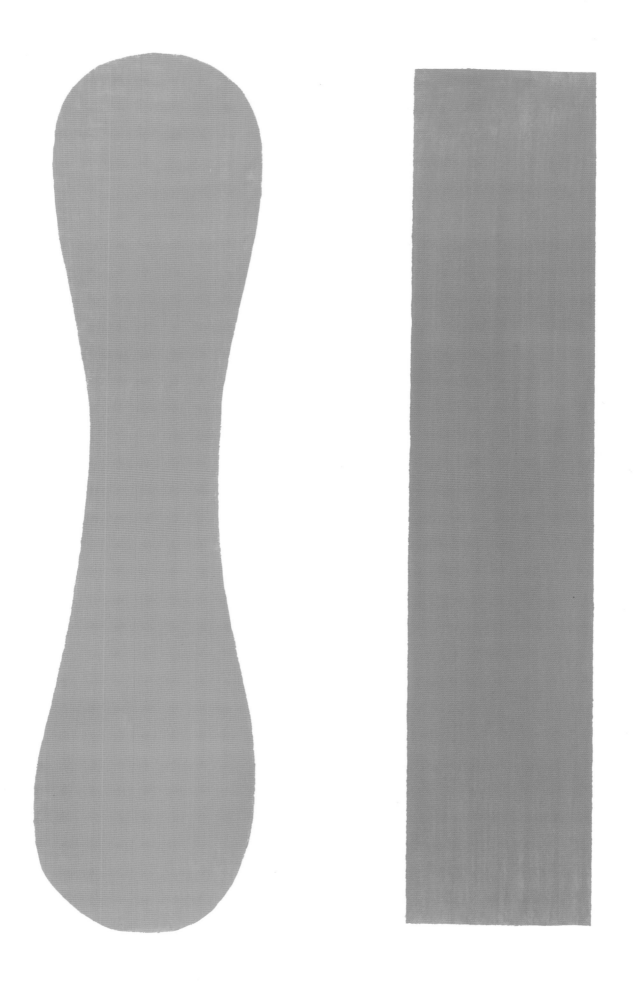

H

J

K

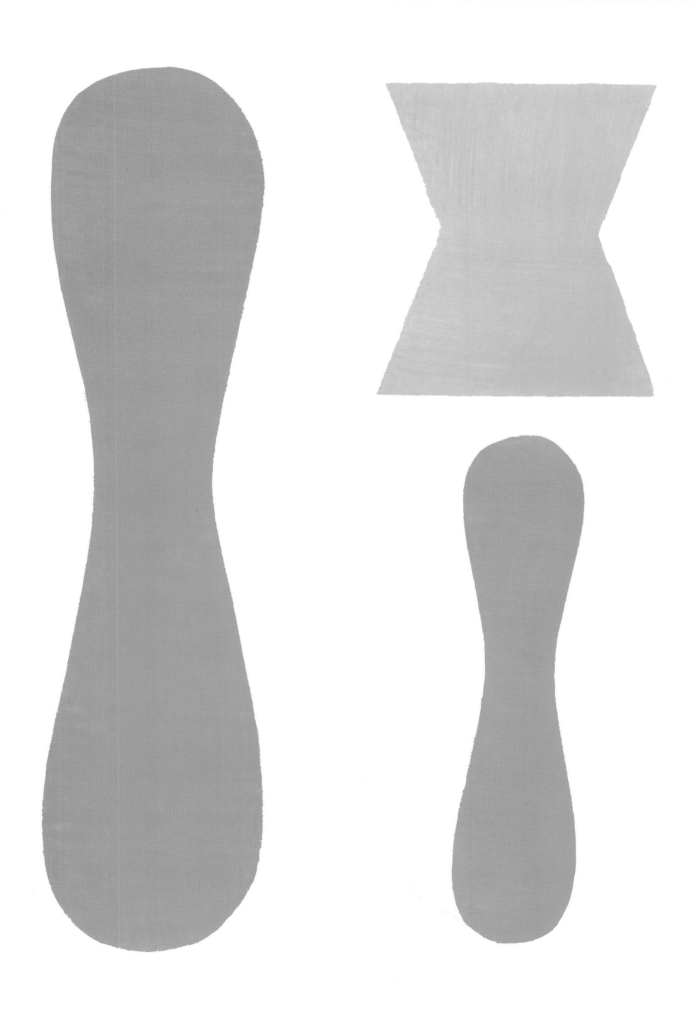

L

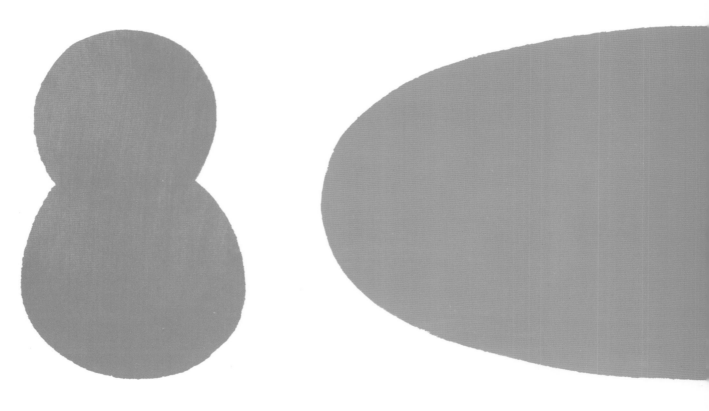

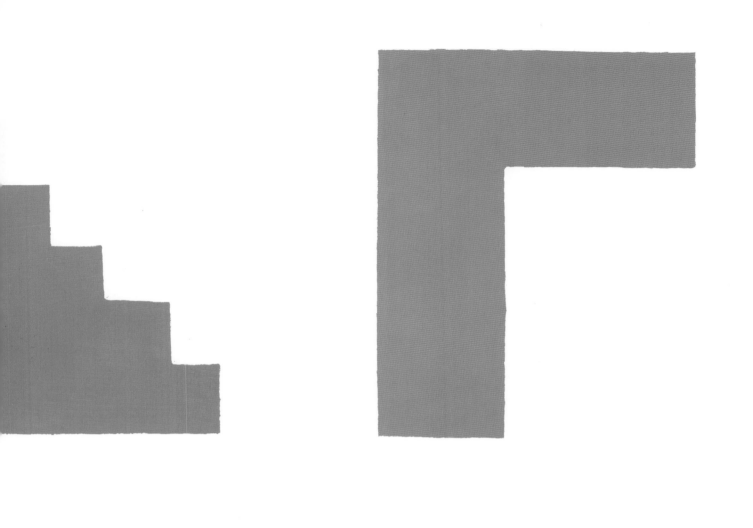
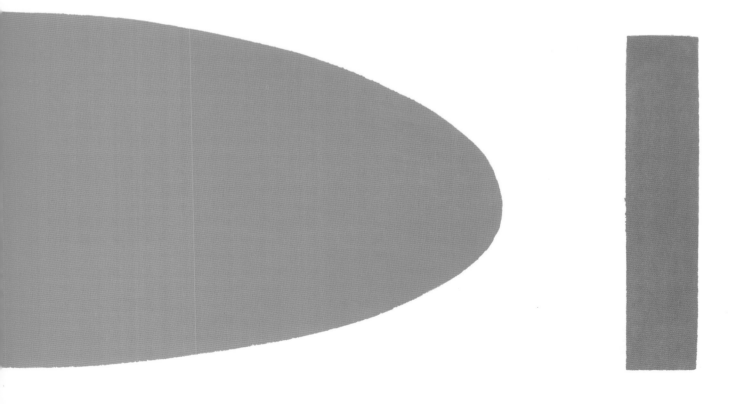

M

P

Q

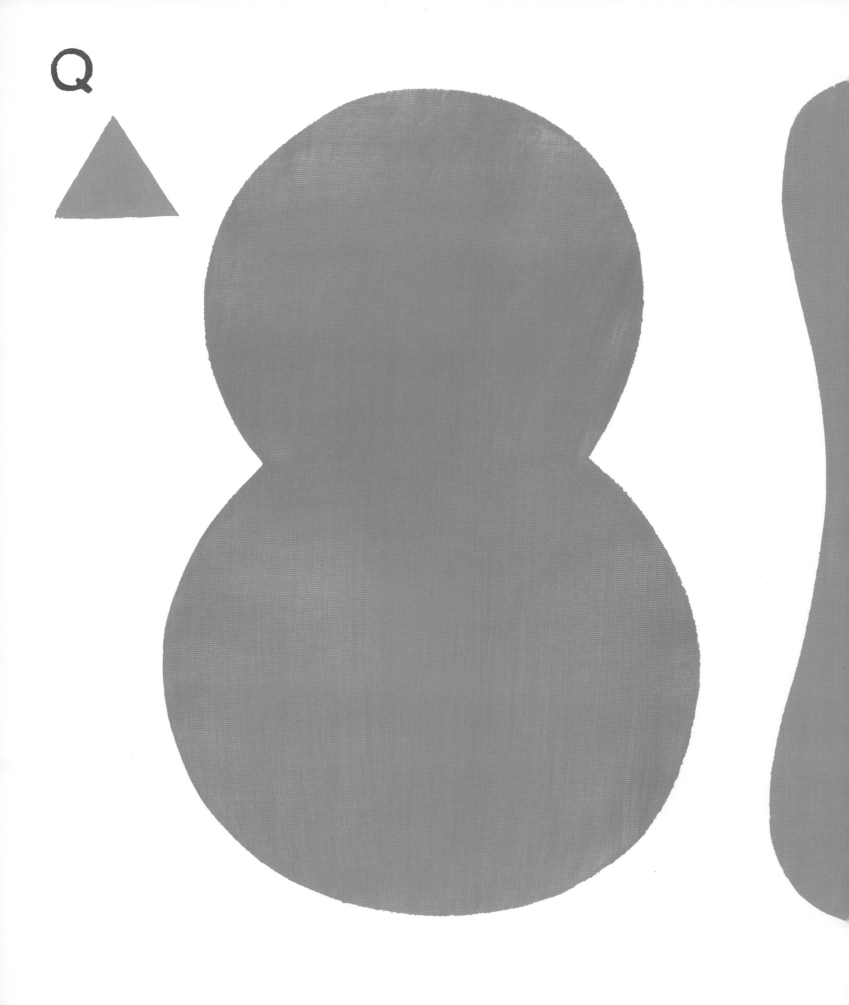

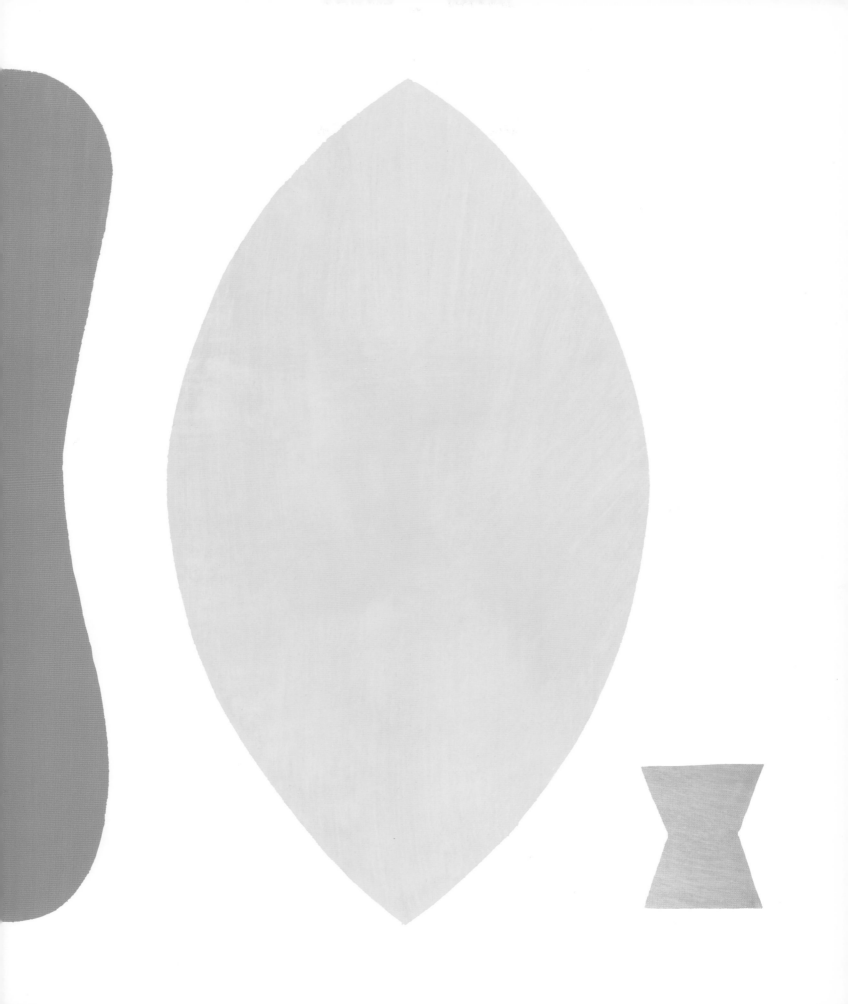

R

S

T

U

V

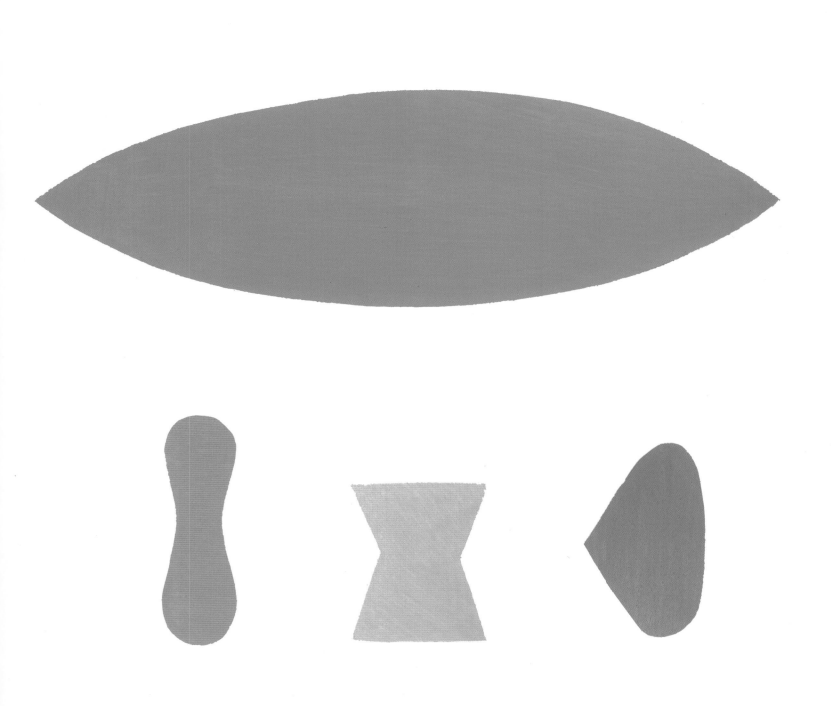

X

Y

z

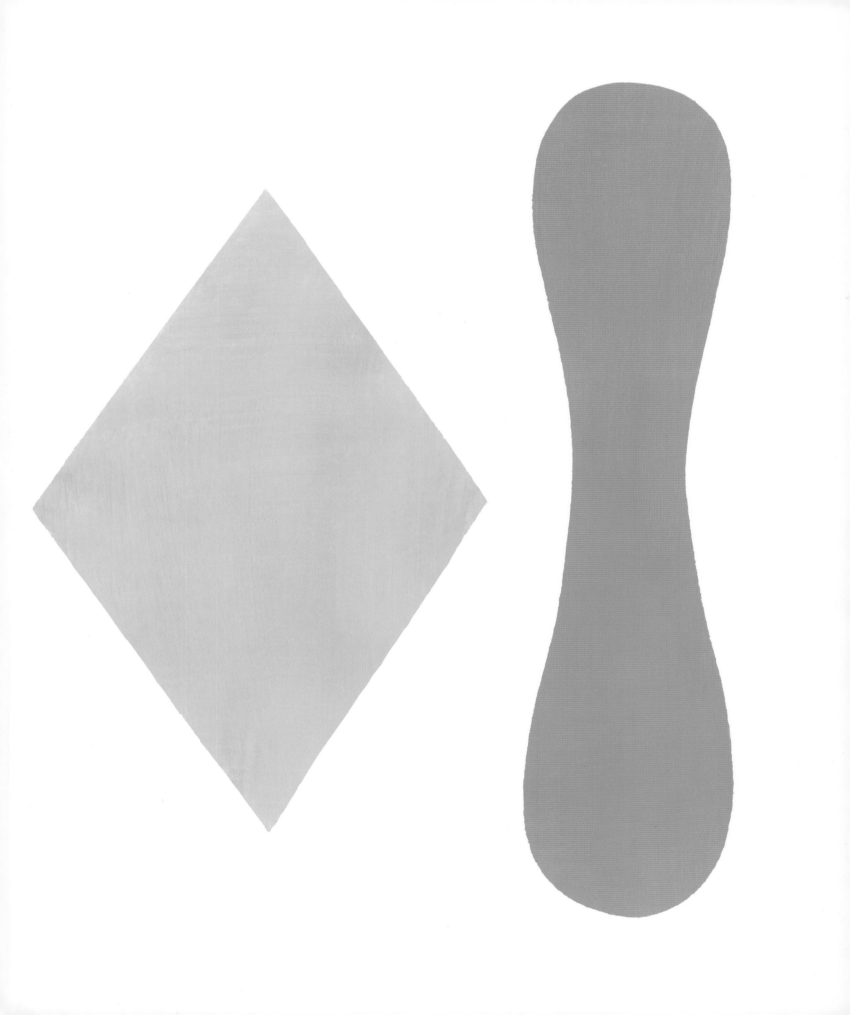